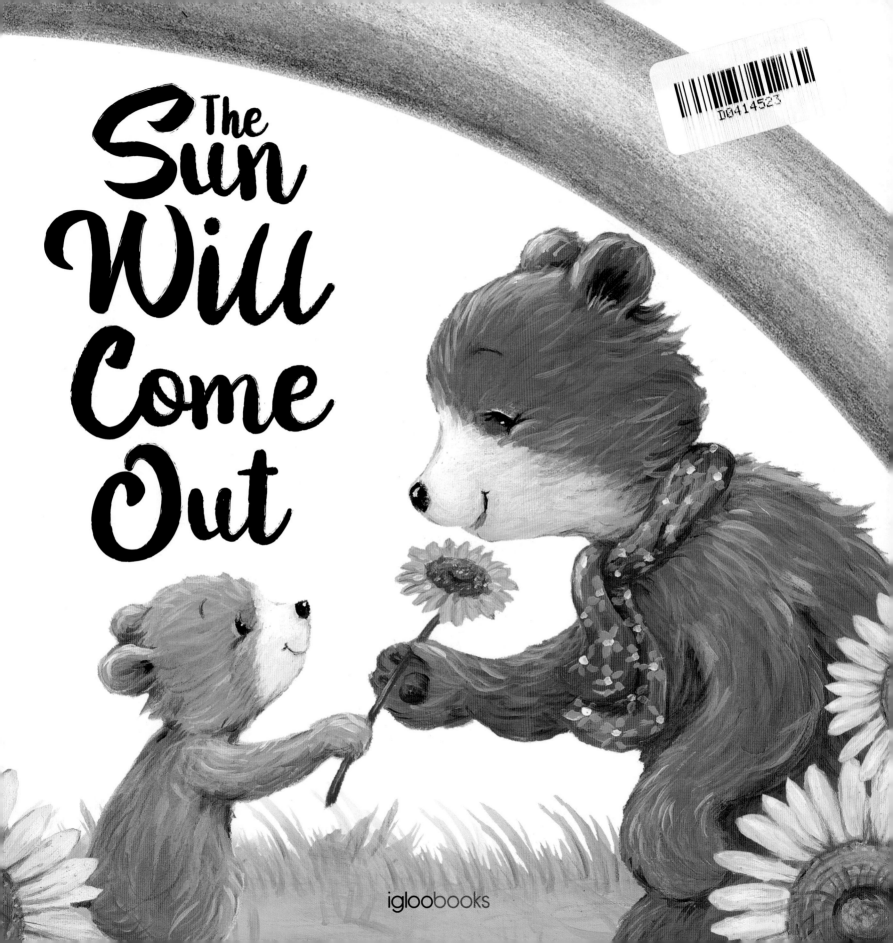

The Sun Will Come Out

igloobooks

If you're feeling worried, or maybe scared or sad...

This igloo book belongs to:

....

igloobooks

Published in 2020
by Igloo Books Ltd
Cottage Farm
Sywell
NN6 0BJ
www.igloobooks.com

Written by Stephanie Moss
Illustrated by Cee Biscoe

Designed by Alex Alexandrou
Edited by Claire Mowat

0520 001
2 4 6 8 10 9 7 5 3 1
ISBN 978-1-83852-217-9

Printed and manufactured in China

... look a little closer.
Lots of good things come from bad!

You can't splish-splosh in puddles
without some drizzly rain.

A cuddle feels
fantastic...

... when it hugs
away your pain.

Ice cream tastes so scrummy when you've finished your whole plate.

Making up with your best friend
feels super-duper great!

It's okay to cry. Your smile won't disappear.

You'll feel brave and happy when you face your biggest fear!

Cosy is more snuggly
when you've been out in the cold.

You might get a great new toy
if one you love is old!

If you scrape
your knee when
you fall down on
the ground...

... you'll forget about it
when you're up, running around!

You can't have your birthday...

... if you don't wait a whole year.

You can rip open your gifts
when the day is finally here!

You think that you hate bedtime each and every single night.

But you love it when I kiss your head
and tuck you in so tight.

The sweetest soothing lullabies come after big bad dreams.

And darkness has to fall for the goodnight stars to gleam.

So whatever happens
there will be a brand-new day.

And you might see a rainbow
when the clouds all fade away.